# There Was an Old Mummy Who Swallowed a Spider

by
## Jennifer Ward

illustrated by
## Steve Gray

two lions

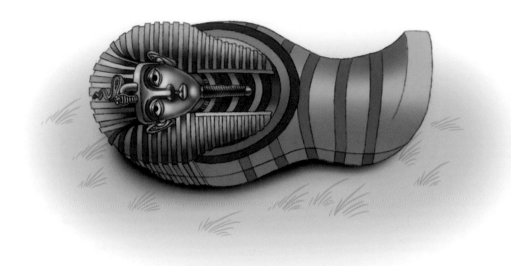

**two lions**

Published by Two Lions, New York
www.apub.com

Amazon, the Amazon logo, and Two Lions are trademarks
of Amazon.com, Inc., or its affiliates.

Library of Congress Control Number: 2014915913

ISBN-13: 9781477826379
ISBN-10: 1477826378

The illustrations are rendered in digital media.
Book design by Vera Soki

Printed in China

First Edition

For Josef Paul.
~J.W.

For Cindy.
Thanks for my happy life.
~S.G.

who swallowed a spider.

I don't know why he swallowed the spider.

Open wider!

There was an old mummy
who swallowed a rat.

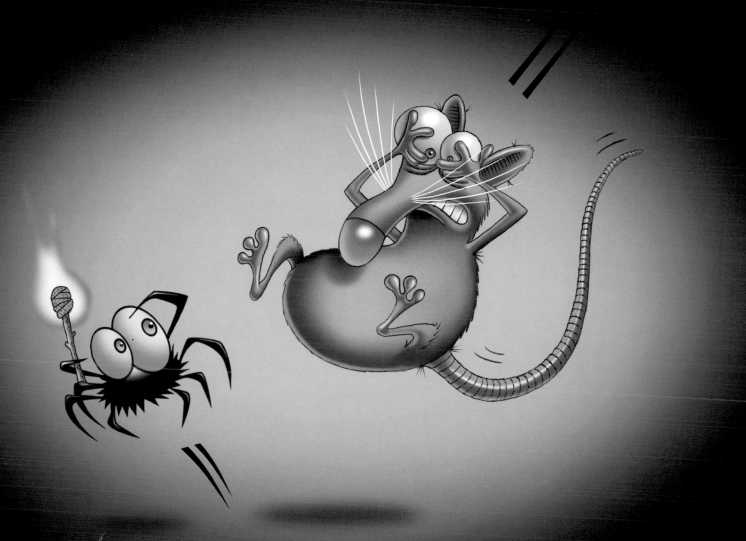

Just like that! Down went the rat.

He swallowed the rat to chase the spider.
I don't know why he swallowed the spider.

Open wider!

There was an old mummy . . .

He swallowed the crow to poke the rat.
He swallowed the rat to chase the spider.
I don't know why he swallowed the spider.

There was an old mummy . . .

who swallowed a bone.
It made him **moan**
to swallow that bone.

He swallowed the bone right after the crow.
He swallowed the crow to poke the rat.
He swallowed the rat to chase the spider.
I don't know why he swallowed the spider.

Open wider!

There was an old mummy . . .

who swallowed some brew.
His belly grew
as he swallowed that brew.

He swallowed the brew to splash the bone.
He swallowed the bone right after the crow.
He swallowed the crow to poke the rat.
He swallowed the rat to chase the spider.
I don't know why he swallowed the spider.

Open wider!

There was an old mummy . . .

who swallowed a witch.
She made him twitch,
that cackling witch.

He swallowed the witch to stir the brew.
He swallowed the brew to splash the bone.
He swallowed the bone right after the crow.
He swallowed the crow to poke the rat.
He swallowed the rat to chase the spider.
I don't know why he swallowed the spider.

Open wider!

There was an old mummy ...

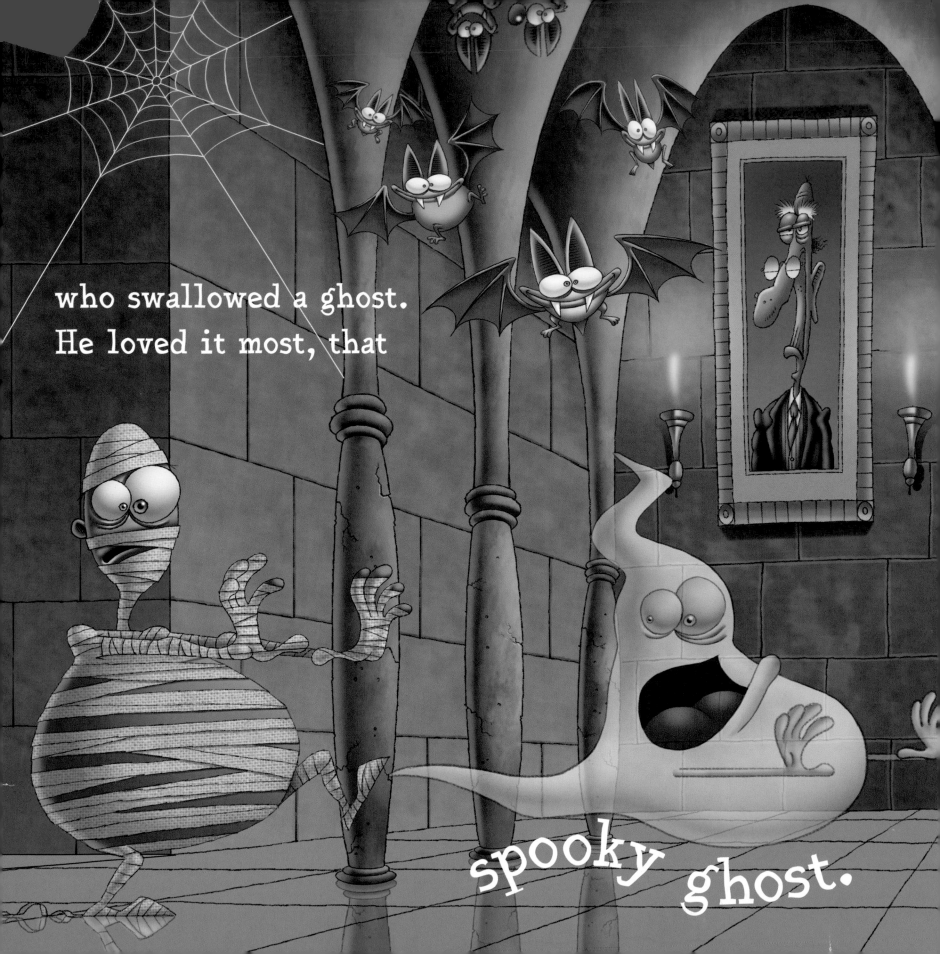

who swallowed a ghost.
He loved it most, that

spooky ghost.

He swallowed the ghost to scare the witch.
He swallowed the witch to stir the brew.
He swallowed the brew to splash the bone.
He swallowed the bone right after the crow.
He swallowed the crow to poke the rat.
He swallowed the rat to chase the spider.
I don't know why he swallowed the spider.

There was an old mummy—
this story is true.
You'd better look out,
or he'll swallow . . .